For Jelena, Mom, Dad, and all bunnies in the world—Anton

Mina, Kian, and Milo—Anne

Anne Ameri-Siemens
Anton Hallmann

Exploring Space

Adventures Across the Universe with Emma and Louis

LITTLE GESTALTEN

Welcome to Space!

Humans have been fascinated by the night sky—and the universe as a whole—for centuries. The stars have always been important guides for people traveling by both land and sea. Looking up at star patterns called constellations helped them find their position and determine whether they should head north, south, east, or west to reach their destination.

Gazing up at the moon and stars also raised lots of questions about the mysteries of the universe. How big is it? How did it all begin? Does the universe stretch out forever? Are there any other forms of life or are humans all alone?

Full of excitement and curiosity, Emma and Louis are about to embark on their latest adventure. They are going to explore the universe! There are huge star systems called galaxies to discover. Some of them are billions of years old, while others have only just formed.

Emma and Louis have prepared for their journey by learning all about different celestial bodies, the force of gravity, and how space travelers experience weightlessness when they leave Earth's protective layer of gases (called the atmosphere) behind. Just like real astronauts, Emma and Louis have had to gather lots of new information and carry out training to be able to go into space. They loved wearing special clothing and equipment in the swimming pool to practice floating in space.

On their mission, they will see for themselves that only a tiny part of the universe is known to us, and that there is no end to the adventures they could have or the discoveries they could make.

Join Emma and Louis on their voyage into space!

What Is the Universe?

When we look up at the dark night sky, space seems to be endless. Yet we can actually only see a tiny fragment of the universe.

It is impossible to imagine just how huge the universe is—it stretches way beyond our planet and includes all the stars, moons, planetary systems, galaxies, gigantic clouds of gas and dust, and even black holes!

Why is the universe so dark and cold when the sun gives off so much heat?

SUN

EARTH

The universe contains everything that exists—matter, energy, space, and time. There are trillions of stars. A trillion has 12 zeros—that's 1,000,000,000,000. There are also big chunks of rock that fly through the universe. They're called asteroids.

Light in space comes from stars such as our sun and from other shining celestial bodies. There are often huge distances between the stars, so wherever starlight fails to reach it is dark and cold. The atmospheres of many celestial bodies, including the planets Earth, Venus, and Saturn, reflect and scatter light from our sun, spreading it further around the universe. Their atmospheres consist of gases that scatter the sunlight. Celestial bodies without an atmosphere (like our moon), or with a very thin atmosphere (like the planet Mercury), reflect light but do not scatter it.

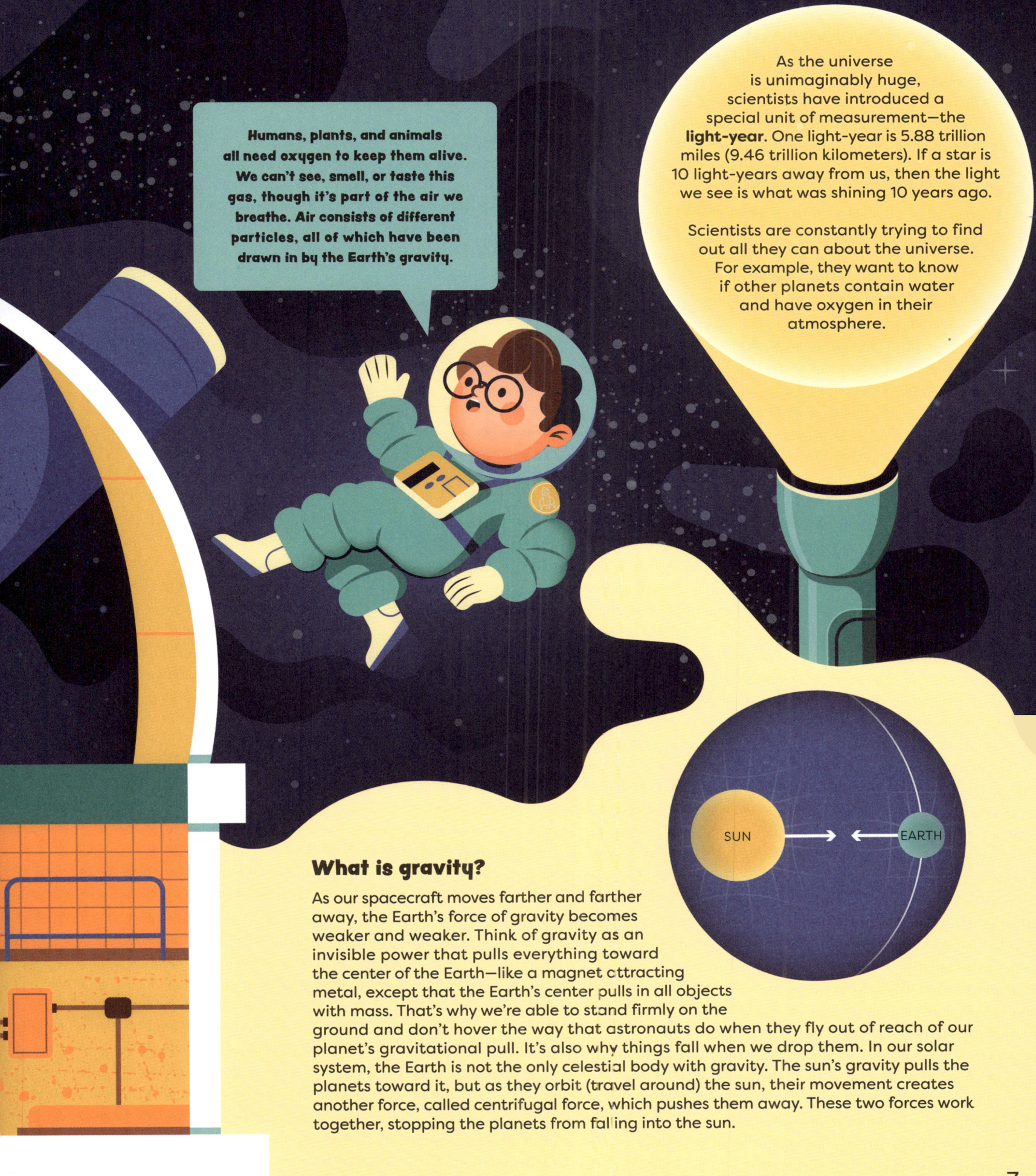

Humans, plants, and animals all need oxygen to keep them alive. We can't see, smell, or taste this gas, though it's part of the air we breathe. Air consists of different particles, all of which have been drawn in by the Earth's gravity.

As the universe is unimaginably huge, scientists have introduced a special unit of measurement—the **light-year**. One light-year is 5.88 trillion miles (9.46 trillion kilometers). If a star is 10 light-years away from us, then the light we see is what was shining 10 years ago.

Scientists are constantly trying to find out all they can about the universe. For example, they want to know if other planets contain water and have oxygen in their atmosphere.

SUN → ← EARTH

What is gravity?

As our spacecraft moves farther and farther away, the Earth's force of gravity becomes weaker and weaker. Think of gravity as an invisible power that pulls everything toward the center of the Earth—like a magnet attracting metal, except that the Earth's center pulls in all objects with mass. That's why we're able to stand firmly on the ground and don't hover the way that astronauts do when they fly out of reach of our planet's gravitational pull. It's also why things fall when we drop them. In our solar system, the Earth is not the only celestial body with gravity. The sun's gravity pulls the planets toward it, but as they orbit (travel around) the sun, their movement creates another force, called centrifugal force, which pushes them away. These two forces work together, stopping the planets from falling into the sun.

The Big Bang Theory

Most scientists believe that the universe began 13.8 billion years ago with a major event known as the big bang.

According to the big bang theory, the whole universe was originally contained in a tiny bubble. The inside was incredibly hot, and everything within it was tightly compressed. Suddenly it all began to expand and the bubble grew bigger and bigger. Imagine inflating a balloon—that was how the universe expanded.

So far, there is no clear proof of how the universe came into being. There is a lot to be said for it and against it: it is a theory.

Around 100–200 million years after the big bang, the first stars were formed from atoms. They shone brightly in the sky. The first galaxies—vast collections of stars, gas, and dust—were formed later, over the course of billions of years after the big bang.

As time went on, the universe expanded more and more. After 380,000 years, tiny particles called atoms began to join together. Imagine atoms as the smallest building blocks—they combined to form the stars, planets, and moons. Everything in our universe is made from atoms!

The American **Edwin Hubble** (1889–1953) was a famous astronomer (a scientist who studies celestial objects). He realized our galaxy, which is named the Milky Way, was only one of many galaxies. Using special equipment, he studied the structure of different galaxies and was able to prove that our universe was expanding. Hubble developed a formula using a figure known as the **Hubble Constant** to determine the speed at which galaxies are moving away from one another. His research was important for the development of the big bang theory.

Another famous scientist, named **Albert Einstein** (1879–1955), viewed the universe as having more than the three dimensions of length, width, and height (as in a room), and added a fourth dimension—time. This allowed a more accurate description of the universe, because it's constantly expanding. Other physicists have continued to investigate the concept of space-time.

Four dimensions

Dimensions are just the different facets of what we can see. When you draw a picture, it will have two dimensions—both length and width. Yet if you draw a simple line, it only has one dimension—length.

1D
ONE-DIMENSIONAL

Only length and no width—one dimension.

2D
TWO-DIMENSIONAL

Adding another line gives the object width, making it two-dimensional.

3D
THREE-DIMENSIONAL

Adding a third line gives it depth—so it's something like a cuboid.

4D
FOUR-DIMENSIONAL

The idea of the fourth dimension is hypothetical and can be discussed spatially (its place in space) or non-spatially (in time).

Our Solar System

Around 4.6 billion years ago, our solar system formed in the universe from a gigantic cloud of gas and dust.

The sun lies at the center of our solar system. That's why it's known as the central star. It has a very powerful gravitational pull, which is why the planets and other celestial bodies circle it.

Mercury is the planet closest to the sun. During the day, the temperature on the surface can rise to over 800 degrees Fahrenheit (427 degrees Celsius). The highest temperature ever recorded on Earth is much lower—around 134 degrees Fahrenheit (57 degrees Celsius).

Comets are large chunks of ice, frozen gases, and particles of dust. When they get close to the sun, the heat makes them change, creating a shiny tail that we can sometimes see from Earth. The tails can be millions of miles long.

Venus is the brightest planet we can see in our sky, because its thick cover of clouds reflects almost 80 percent of the sun's light. Only the moon is brighter.

The surface of **Mars** contains a lot of iron oxide, which gives it a reddish color. The planet is covered with craters, volcanoes, desert landscapes, and icy polar regions of frozen water and frozen carbon dioxide.

Earth and the planets Mercury, Venus, and Mars have one thing in common— they're all composed of rock and metal. The planets Jupiter, Saturn, Uranus, and Neptune are made mainly of gas.

The Earth is still the only planet that we know supports life.

SUN

SATURN

URANUS

JUPITER

VENUS

MARS

MERCURY

EARTH

NEPTUNE

Size of the planets compared to the sun

The diameter (length across) of **Saturn** is around nine times that of the Earth. Around the planet, different-sized pieces of ice and rocks swirl—some are as large as a car and others are as small as a grain of sand. They are all drawn in by Saturn's gravitational pull, forming distinctive rings as they orbit the planet.

The largest planet in our solar system is **Jupiter**. It's orbited by about 95 moons, one of which is called Ganymede. It's even bigger than the planet Mercury.

The distances between the sun and the planets change. This is because their orbits around the sun are not circular, but oval-shaped—like a chicken's egg. So the distances between the Earth and the other planets also change.

The telescope

For many centuries, people believed that the Earth was the center of the universe and all the other celestial bodies, including the sun, moved around it. Galileo Galilei changed our view of the universe forever. In 1610, the great astronomer used a new instrument— the telescope. He wanted to observe Jupiter, and he saw four moons circling the planet. This proved to him that other celestial bodies did not move around the Earth.

The planet **Uranus** is surrounded by methane, a gas that reflects blue light. This gives it its bluish hue.

Neptune is the outermost planet in our solar system. While the Earth orbits the sun in 365 days, it takes Neptune 165 years.

There is a saying to memorize the order of the the planets from closest to farthest from the sun—**M**y **V**ery **E**xcellent **M**other **J**ust **S**erved **U**s **N**oodles. The first letter of each word stands for one of the planets!

The Sun

The sun is around 4.6 billion years old. It's the largest star in our solar system.

The Earth orbits the sun, completing a full circuit in 365 days. As it does so, it rotates on its own axis. The side facing the sun has daylight, while the opposite side has night.

Earth is much smaller than the sun—you could fit around 1.3 million Earths inside it!

Diameter: 865,000 mi (1.4 million km)
Length of day: 25 Earth days
Length of year: The solar system (including the sun) takes 225–250 million years to orbit the center of the Milky Way
Distance from Earth: 93 million mi (150 million km)

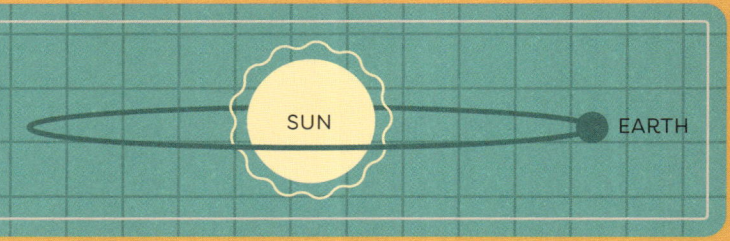

SUN   EARTH

The sun is a giant ball of gas and plasma. Plasma is like gas but it has supercharged particles bouncing around. The sun's interior temperature reaches around 27 million degrees Fahrenheit (15 million degrees Celsius), while its surface temperature ranges between 9,900 and 10,800 degrees Fahrenheit (5,500 and 6,000 degrees Celsius). That kind of heat is scarcely imaginable for us!

By comparison, water boils at 212 degrees Fahrenheit (100 degrees Celsius). That means the surface of the sun is around 60 times hotter than boiling water.

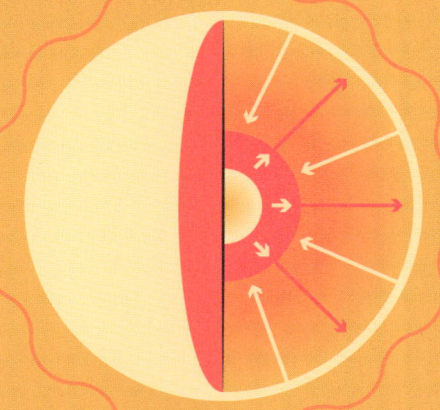

The sun sends out gas and plasma in the form of gigantic, glowing waves. These are known as prominences, some of which can be larger than the Earth.

Inside the sun

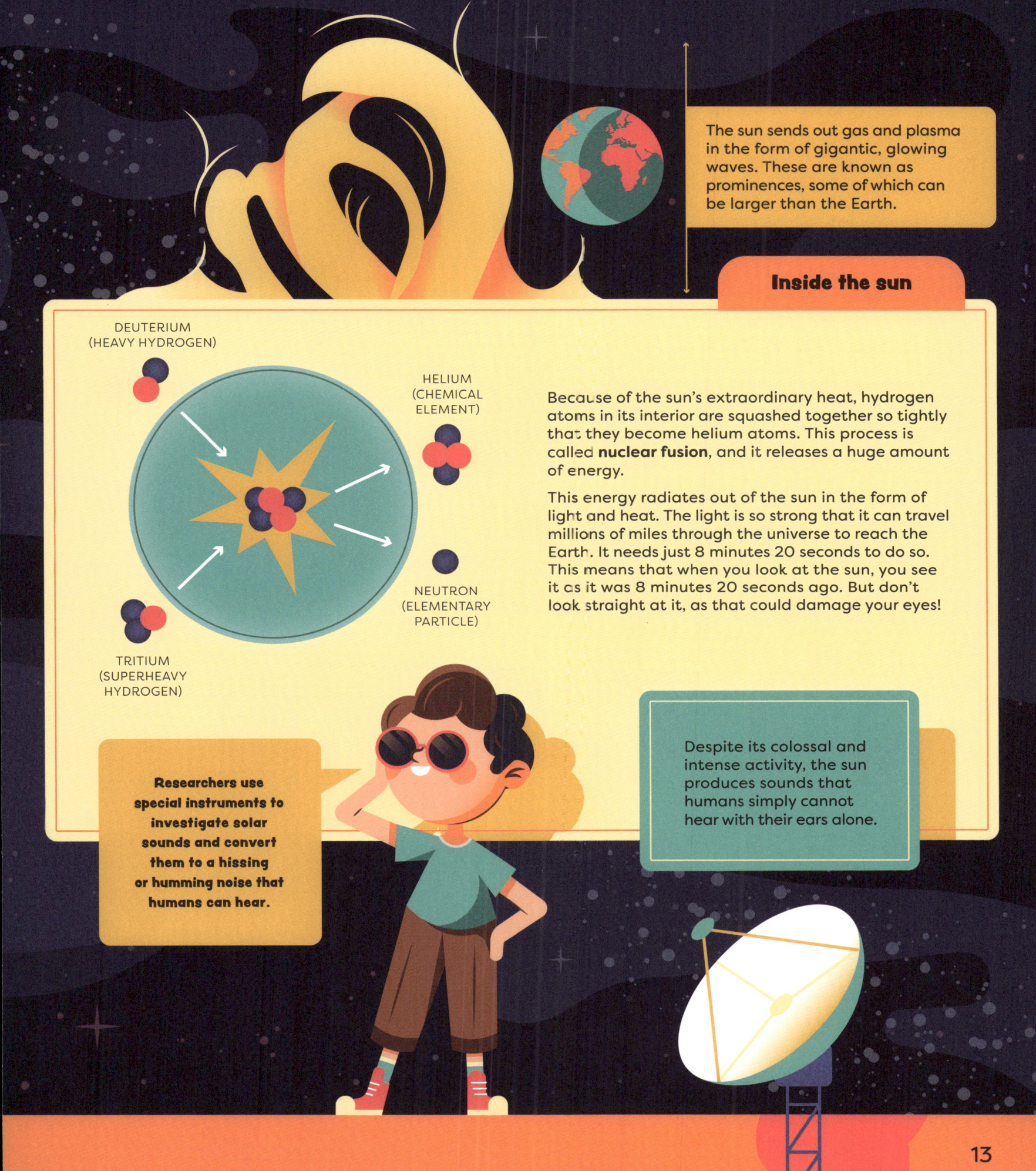

DEUTERIUM
(HEAVY HYDROGEN)

HELIUM
(CHEMICAL ELEMENT)

NEUTRON
(ELEMENTARY PARTICLE)

TRITIUM
(SUPERHEAVY HYDROGEN)

Because of the sun's extraordinary heat, hydrogen atoms in its interior are squashed together so tightly that they become helium atoms. This process is called **nuclear fusion**, and it releases a huge amount of energy.

This energy radiates out of the sun in the form of light and heat. The light is so strong that it can travel millions of miles through the universe to reach the Earth. It needs just 8 minutes 20 seconds to do so. This means that when you look at the sun, you see it as it was 8 minutes 20 seconds ago. But don't look straight at it, as that could damage your eyes!

Researchers use special instruments to investigate solar sounds and convert them to a hissing or humming noise that humans can hear.

Despite its colossal and intense activity, the sun produces sounds that humans simply cannot hear with their ears alone.

The Earth

The Earth is the only planet on which life is known to exist, thanks to the presence of air, water, and carbon-based molecules that together form our atmosphere.

The blue planet

The Earth is around 4.5 billion years old. From space it looks blue, because 71 percent of its surface is covered with water.

71 %

More than half of the oxygen in the Earth's atmosphere comes from the oceans. The oxygen is mainly produced by plankton and algae.

Our planet has gone through many phases in its history. Around 3.5 billion years ago, the surface was extremely hot and the atmosphere contained various gases, including water vapor. The heat led to continuous rain, and as the Earth cooled, the water gathered on the crust, forming one gigantic ocean. The rain also brought down gases such as carbon dioxide and sulfur from the atmosphere, causing the composition of the air to change.

The first forms of life were tiny cyanobacteria (also known as blue-green algae), and these emerged in the water. They began a process called photosynthesis, which transformed sunlight, water, and carbon dioxide into energy and released oxygen, which they did not need. At first the oxygen remained in the water, but then it rose up into the Earth's atmosphere.

Diameter: 7,918mi (12,742km)
Length of day: 24 hours
Length of year: 365.25 days
Distance from the sun: 93 million mi (150 million km)

i

Rotations

When we stand on the surface of the Earth, it doesn't feel like it is moving. However our planet is not only orbiting the sun, it is also spinning on its own axis at a speed of 1,039 miles per hour (1,670 kilometers per hour). A full rotation takes 24 hours (one day). As one side of the Earth is always facing the sun, the light changes throughout the day. This creates the cycle of days and nights.

Earth's atmosphere

The atmosphere is the layer of air that surrounds our planet. It consists of five layers:

The outermost layer of the Earth's atmosphere is the **exosphere**, where the transition to outer space is smooth and it is incredibly hot: 1,832°F (1,000°C)!

The **thermosphere** extends from the mesosphere to a height of around 310 miles (500 kilometers). Auroras (beautiful colored lights in the night sky) can occur in this layer.

The **mesosphere** is the third layer of the Earth's atmosphere, where it is as cold as -130°F (-95°C).

The **stratosphere** contains the ozone layer, which protects us from harmful **ultraviolet radiation** from the sun.

The **troposphere** is the lowest layer of the atmosphere, where all our weather takes place.

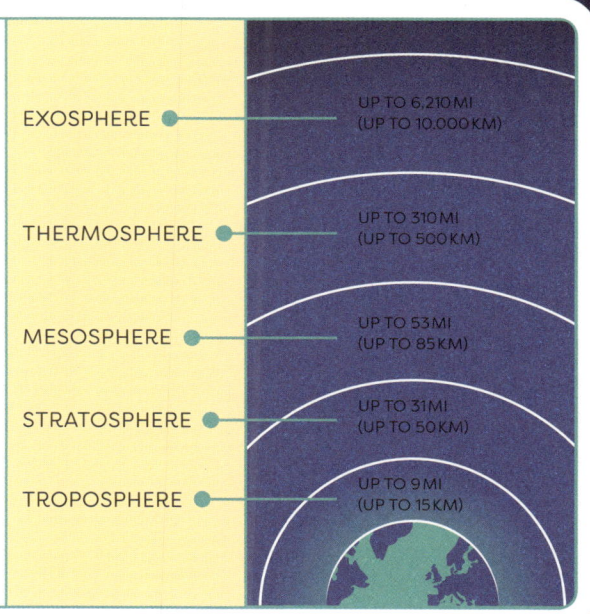

EXOSPHERE — UP TO 6,210 MI (UP TO 10,000 KM)

THERMOSPHERE — UP TO 310 MI (UP TO 500 KM)

MESOSPHERE — UP TO 53 MI (UP TO 85 KM)

STRATOSPHERE — UP TO 31 MI (UP TO 50 KM)

TROPOSPHERE — UP TO 9 MI (UP TO 15 KM)

Our Moon

We can see the moon shining at night, but it doesn't emit any light of its own. We can only see it because it's illuminated by the sun.

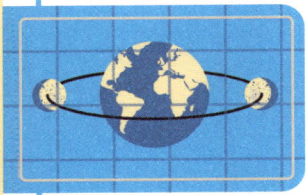

The moon is mostly made of rock, with a crust containing minerals that are also found in the Earth's crust.

It takes around three days for a rocket to fly from the Earth to the moon. This would be the equivalent of a nonstop car journey lasting almost six months.

Moons are celestial bodies that orbit planets. They're known as natural satellites. The Earth only has one moon, but some other planets in our solar system have several. Mercury and Venus have no moons at all.

In 1959, the Soviet Luna 3 probe became the first mission without crew to send back pictures of the far side of the moon.
In 1968, the US crew of the Apollo 8 mission became the first humans to see the far side.
In 2019, the Chinese Chang'e 4 mission achieved the first landing on the far side.

The moon orbits the Earth once a month—every 29.53 days. This period of time is known as the **moon phase cycle**. During the cycle, different amounts of the moon are visible, depending on its position relative to the sun as it orbits the Earth.

At **full moon**, the sun is shining directly on the side facing the Earth. During the **new moon**, there is no sunlight on the side of the moon that is facing the Earth. When the moon is illuminated from the side, it can look like a slice of cake!

The side of the moon that remains hidden from the Earth is known as the dark side of the moon.

WANING HALF MOON

WANING CRESCENT MOON

WANING THREE-QUARTER MOON

NEW MOON

FULL MOON

WAXING CRESCENT MOON

WAXING THREE-QUARTER MOON

WAXING HALF MOON

Moon crater

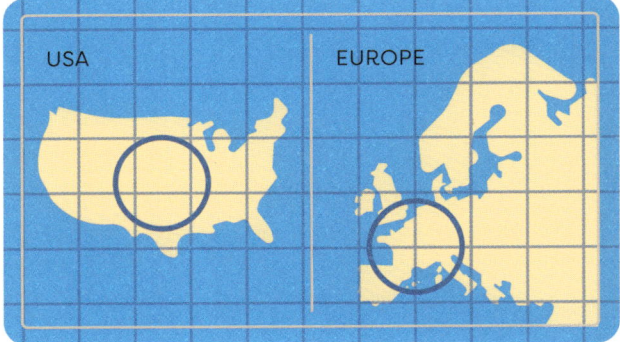

USA

EUROPE

The largest crater on the moon is called the **South Pole-Aitken Basin**. Its diameter is 1,392 miles (2,240 kilometers)—About the size of a quarter of the USA or several European countries would fit inside.

Diameter: 2,159 mi (3,474 km)
Length of day: 29.5 Earth days
Length of year: 365 Earth days
Distance from the sun: 93 million mi
(150 million km)
Closest distance from Earth:
236,121 mi (380,000 km)

Lava plains

At first, scientists thought that the dark areas we can see on the moon were oceans. They named them "mare" or "maria" as *mare* is Latin for sea. In fact, these patches are giant plains made of cooled lava called basalt. At the time the dinosaurs roamed the Earth—they died out 65 million years ago—there were still active volcanoes on the moon.

The South Pole

The moon's South Pole is very cold. There's frozen water in its deep craters, which could potentially be used to make rocket fuel for future space probes.

The name we give to the dust that forms on the surface of rocky moons and planets is "regolith." This rocky dust consists of several different materials.

The moon's surface is covered with a thick layer of fine grey dust created by volcanic eruptions and meteorite (space rock) collisions. The moon dust has lots of sharp edges, which could easily damage the space suits worn by astronauts. This danger is why it is so important for space scientists to improve the protective equipment used on space missions.

Mars

Mars is also known as the Red Planet because its rocky surface contains a lot of iron. When iron rusts it turns a reddish color—just like Mars.

Structure

Just like Earth, Mars consists of two parts called hemispheres, with a North Pole at the top and a South Pole at the bottom. The northern hemisphere is much flatter and smoother than the southern one.

The ice caps on Mars are mainly made up of frozen water and carbon dioxide. Scientists believe that the planet's surface may have been covered by glaciers (large masses of ice) until a few million years ago.

It has a frozen lake that is around 150 feet (45 meters) deep and is thought to be as large as the Earth's North Sea.

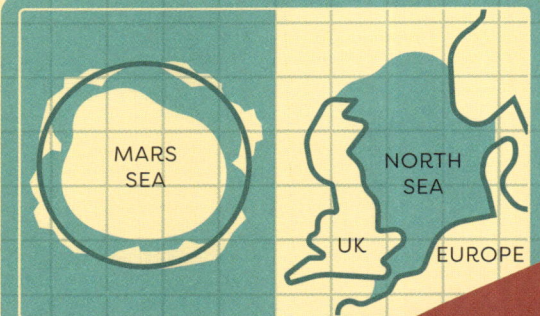

MARS SEA

NORTH SEA

UK

EUROPE

Moons

Mars has two moons, Phobos and Deimos. It is likely that they came from asteroids or debris around Mars. Phobos's lumpy shape makes it look more like an asteroid. It measures 17 miles (27 kilometers) across.

Olympus Mons

On Mars there is a volcano 16 miles (25 kilometers) high, named Olympus Mons. It's the highest mountain and the largest volcano in our solar system.

The atmosphere on Mars is made up mainly of carbon dioxide and just a small amount of oxygen (0.13 percent). On Earth the amount of oxygen in the air is 21 percent. Humans would only be able to breathe on Mars if they had special equipment.

Diameter: 4,222 mi (6,794 km)
Length of day: 24 hours 37 minutes—
a day on Mars is called a sol
Length of year: around two Earth years
Average distance from the sun:
142 million mi (228 million km)
Closest distance from Earth:
33.9 million mi (54.6 million km)

Temperatures and seasons

During the day, temperatures on Mars can reach more than 68 degrees Fahrenheit (20 degrees Celsius) at its equator—the invisible line around the middle of the planet. However, at night, temperatures drop to as low as -112 degrees Fahrenheit (-80 degrees Celsius).

Just like planet Earth's, Mars has seasons. They last much longer than ours because Mars takes longer to orbit the sun.

Mars also experiences weather phenomena similar to Earth, for example dust storms that can move at speeds of more than 63 miles per hour (100 kilometers per hour). However, rain never falls because its atmosphere cannot hold water vapor from which rain could form.

The US space agency NASA and other countries' space agencies have launched 50 missions to Mars. One was the Rover Curiosity (more on page 45), which used robots to explore the planet. So far, no humans have ever set foot on Mars, but it may not be long before someone takes the first step!

Craters

The **Valles Marineris** is a canyon system about 4.35 miles (7 kilometers) deep, 2,500 miles (4,000 kilometers) long, and 125 miles (200 kilometers) wide. NASA calculates that there are more than 43,000 craters of this type on Mars.

VALLES MARINERIS, 124 MI (200 KM)

GRAND CANYON 16 MI (26 KM)

Jupiter

Jupiter is the largest planet in our solar system and is mainly made up of gases like helium and hydrogen. That is why it is called a gas giant.

Incredible cold

The surface of Jupiter is very cold, averaging -148 degrees Fahrenheit (-100 degrees Celsius). This is because the planet's outer layers of gas and clouds are extremely thick and do not allow any heat to pass through. Another reason for the extreme cold is: Jupiter is very far away from the sun. It therefore receives very little sunlight.

Of all the planets in our solar system, Jupiter has the shortest days because it rotates so quickly on its own axis...

Cosmic vacuum cleaner

Jupiter's strong gravity acts like a magnet, pulling rocks and asteroids away from Earth's path. This protects us from potential collisions. Jupiter is often called a "cosmic vacuum cleaner" because of the way it helps clear the space around us.

...because Jupiter is so fast, its clouds look like stripes to the human eye.

Galileo and the moons

As well as being a gas giant, Jupiter has lots of moons orbiting around it! There are at least 95, but there could be more. The four biggest are called the **Galilean moons** because they were discovered in 1610 by Galileo Galilei.

Io is the most active volcanic celestial body in our solar system, and is the innermost of Jupiter's four largest moons.

Europa is covered by a layer of thick ice. Scientists believe there is salt water underneath the ice. This area is believed to be about 62 miles (100 kilometers) deep. This would equal the same amount of water in all the Earth's oceans combined.

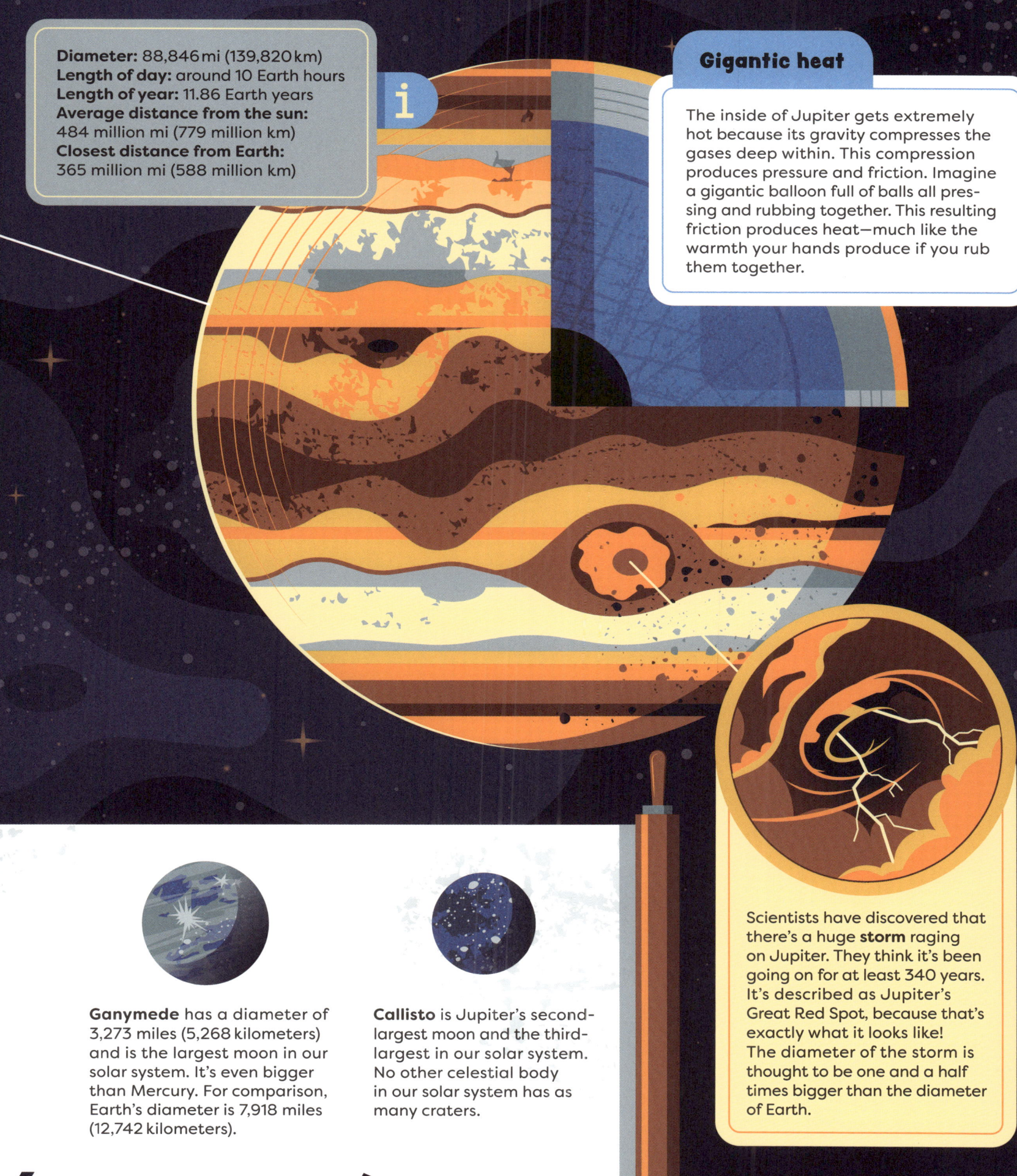

Diameter: 88,846 mi (139,820 km)
Length of day: around 10 Earth hours
Length of year: 11.86 Earth years
Average distance from the sun:
484 million mi (779 million km)
Closest distance from Earth:
365 million mi (588 million km)

Gigantic heat

The inside of Jupiter gets extremely hot because its gravity compresses the gases deep within. This compression produces pressure and friction. Imagine a gigantic balloon full of balls all pressing and rubbing together. This resulting friction produces heat—much like the warmth your hands produce if you rub them together.

Ganymede has a diameter of 3,273 miles (5,268 kilometers) and is the largest moon in our solar system. It's even bigger than Mercury. For comparison, Earth's diameter is 7,918 miles (12,742 kilometers).

Callisto is Jupiter's second-largest moon and the third-largest in our solar system. No other celestial body in our solar system has as many craters.

Scientists have discovered that there's a huge **storm** raging on Jupiter. They think it's been going on for at least 340 years. It's described as Jupiter's Great Red Spot, because that's exactly what it looks like! The diameter of the storm is thought to be one and a half times bigger than the diameter of Earth.

Saturn

Just like Jupiter, Saturn is a gas giant. It is made up of gas and has no solid surface.

Space probes

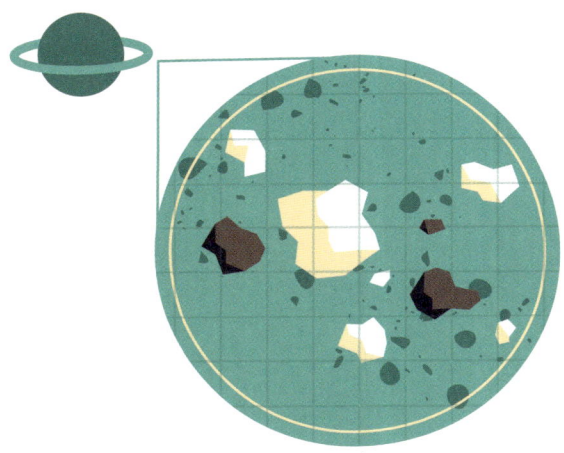

Over the past few decades, various space probes, such as the Cassini-Huygens, Voyager 1, and Voyager 2, have been sent to study Saturn. These probes have transmitted pictures and information back to Earth, revealing that Saturn's rings (as we see them) are made up of thousands of thin rings. Some of these are just a few feet thick but they stretch millions of miles around the planet. They are made up of ice and stone, from microscopic grains to larger chunks.

The tiny particles in Saturn's rings are constantly on the move. They're affected by the planet's gravity. They also attract or repel one another. As a result, the rings expand and even divide themselves up into separate sections and then come together again.

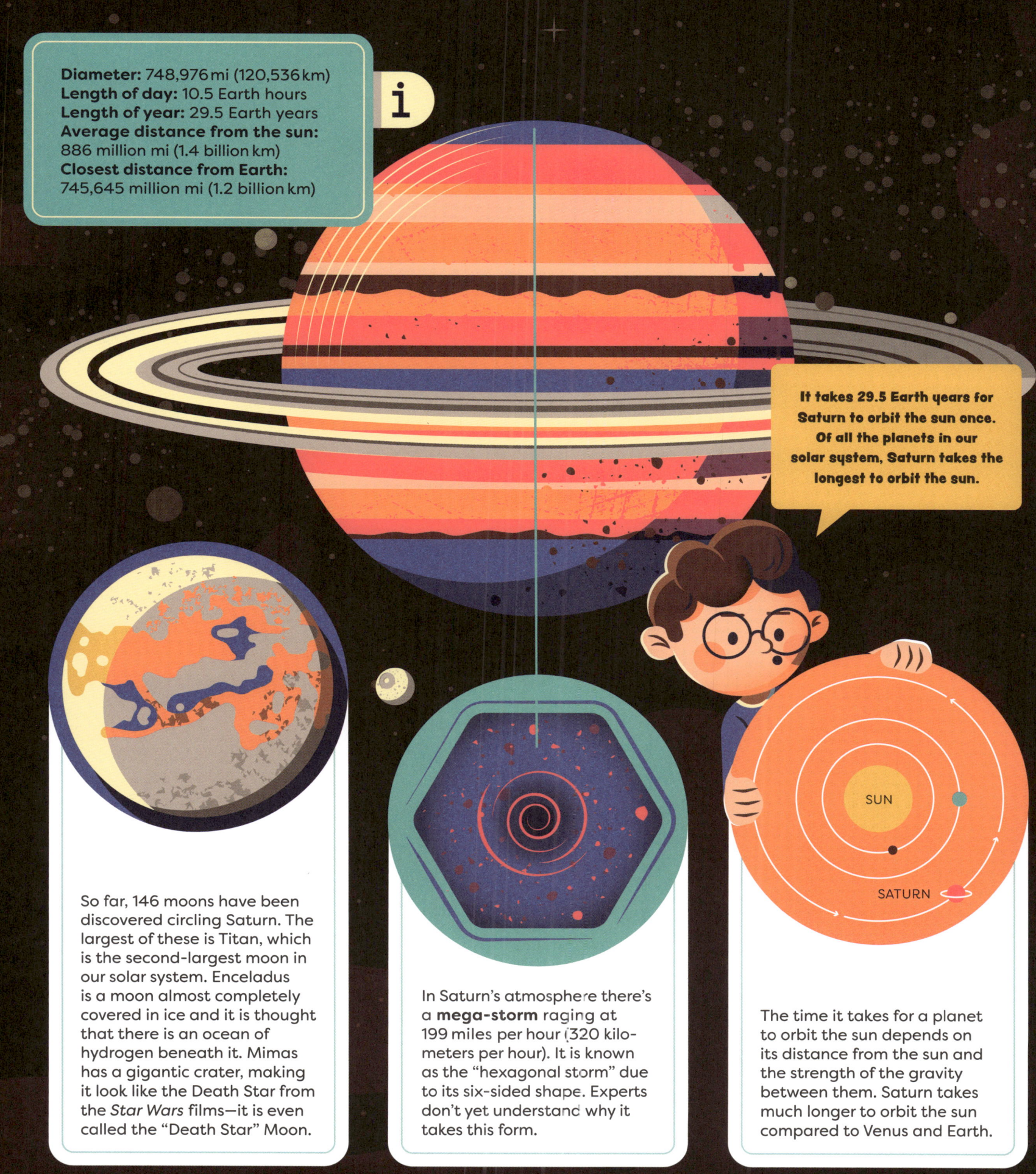

Diameter: 748,976 mi (120,536 km)
Length of day: 10.5 Earth hours
Length of year: 29.5 Earth years
Average distance from the sun:
886 million mi (1.4 billion km)
Closest distance from Earth:
745,645 million mi (1.2 billion km)

It takes 29.5 Earth years for Saturn to orbit the sun once. Of all the planets in our solar system, Saturn takes the longest to orbit the sun.

SUN

SATURN

So far, 146 moons have been discovered circling Saturn. The largest of these is Titan, which is the second-largest moon in our solar system. Enceladus is a moon almost completely covered in ice and it is thought that there is an ocean of hydrogen beneath it. Mimas has a gigantic crater, making it look like the Death Star from the *Star Wars* films—it is even called the "Death Star" Moon.

In Saturn's atmosphere there's a **mega-storm** raging at 199 miles per hour (320 kilometers per hour). It is known as the "hexagonal storm" due to its six-sided shape. Experts don't yet understand why it takes this form.

The time it takes for a planet to orbit the sun depends on its distance from the sun and the strength of the gravity between them. Saturn takes much longer to orbit the sun compared to Venus and Earth.

Neptune

Neptune is the outermost planet in our solar system. It's a shimmering blue and it could be raining diamonds in its atmosphere!

The blue color of Neptune comes from the methane gas in its atmosphere. This gas absorbs the red light and reflects the blue light from the sun. This is why Neptune looks blue.

Beneath its veil of gas, Neptune has a solid core, which consists mainly of rock and metal. It also has rings around it, although these are far less prominent than the famous rings around Saturn.

Diameter: 30,598 mi (49,244 km)
Length of day: 16 Earth hours
Length of year: 165 Earth years
Average distance from the sun:
2.8 billion mi (4.5 billion km)
Closest distance from Earth:
2.7 billion mi (4.3 billion km)

i

So far, **14 moons** have been discovered orbiting Neptune, the largest of which is Triton, which has an average temperature of around -391 degrees Fahrenheit (-235 degrees Celsius). It is the coldest-known place in our solar system.

The average temperature on Neptune is around -353 degrees Fahrenheit (-214 degrees Celsius), because it's so far away from the sun.

Floating Diamonds

There is enormous pressure inside the planet Neptune. Its solid core is encased in a layer of ice. This ice consists mainly of methane, which is made up of carbon and hydrogen. The high pressure could be causing the carbon to split, which could be leading to the formation of diamonds that float into Neptune's deeper layers.

Venus

Venus is the brightest celestial body after the sun and the moon. It is also known as the morning star and evening star, although it is not a star.

A day on Venus is longer than a Venusian year! This is because Venus orbits the sun faster than it rotates on its own axis. At 4 miles per hour (6.5 kilometers per hour), this rotation around its own axis is so slow that Venus needs around 243 Earth days to complete it.

Diameter: 7,521mi (12,104km)
Length of day: 243 Earth days
Length of year: 225 Earth days
Average distance from the sun:
67 million mi (108 million km)
Closest distance from Earth:
38 million mi (61 million km)

The air pressure on Venus is similar to the pressure deep in the ocean on our planet, about 2,950 feet (900 meters) down. Only a few creatures, like some fish, can handle this amount of pressure. However they still wouldn't be able to live on Venus. It is far too hot, there's no water, and the air is mostly carbon dioxide—it wouldn't be possible for them to breathe.

Venus is almost as big as the Earth and is also a rocky planet. This is why it is also known as the Earth's twin.

The temperature on Venus is around 873 degrees Fahrenheit (467 degrees Celsius), making it the hottest planet in our solar system.

Surrounding Venus is a cloud cover that is an incredible 12,5 miles (20 kilometers) thick, and consists primarily of sulfuric acid, which is poisonous. These cloud layers reflect almost 80 percent of the sun's light, and this is the reason why Venus is one of the brightest celestial bodies in our social system.

Mercury

Mercury is the closest planet to our sun. It completes its orbit in just 88 Earth days! Like Earth, Mars, and Venus, Mercury is a rocky planet. It formed around 4.5 billion years ago.

Of all the planets in our solar system, Mercury has the shortest year. This is because it orbits the sun so quickly. There are huge cliffs on Mercury's surface, which are hundreds of feet high and several hundred miles long.

There are countless craters on the surface of Mercury. They originate from meteorite and asteroid impacts and are named after famous personalities—for example, writers such as Mark Twain and the Brontë sisters, composers such as Johann Sebastian Bach, and artists such as Michelangelo.

During the day, the temperature on Mercury can rise to more than 752 degrees Fahrenheit (400 degrees Celsius), and at night it plunges to -274 degrees Fahrenheit (-170 degrees Celsius). Because of the huge differences in temperature, the absence of atmosphere, and the strong solar radiation, life would not be possible on Mercury. The extremes of heat and cold make even the hardest rock crumble.

Mercury is the smallest planet in our solar system.

Diameter: 3,032 mi (4,880 km)
Length of day: 58 Earth days
Length of year: 88 Earth days
Average distance from the sun:
36 million mi (57.9 million km)
Closest distance from Earth:
48 million mi (77 million km)

i

Most planets stand (almost) upright, but Uranus "rolls" around the sun like an upturned spinning top.

The distance between the sun and Uranus is vast! It would be similar to traveling from New York to London more than half a million times.

Uranus

Uranus is one of the gas giants in our solar system. It gives out a blue glow due to the methane gas in its atmosphere. This methane absorbs red sunlight and reflects blue light, like Neptune.

As Uranus leans heavily toward one side, most of the time the sun's rays only reach one half of the planet, so the other half remains in darkness. That's why Uranus alternates between 21 years of winter and 21 years of summer.

So far, **27 moons** have been discovered orbiting Uranus. Two of them—Titania and Oberon—were named after characters from the play *A Midsummer Night's Dream* by the famous English playwright William Shakespeare (1564–1616).

i

Diameter: 31,518 mi (50,724 km)
Length of day: 17 Earth hours
Length of year: 84 Earth years
Average distance from the sun: 1.8 billion mi (2.9 billion km)
Closest distance from Earth: 1.6 billion mi (2.6 billion km)

The Stars

Stars are shining balls of gas that exist throughout the universe. They are the bright, twinkling lights that we see in the night sky.

During the day, when we are on the side of the Earth facing the sun, it appears brighter than all the other stars in the sky. When it gets dark, we can no longer see the sun, but we can see all the other stars.

The second-brightest star (after the sun) that we can see from the Earth is Sirius. It actually consists of two stars and forms a double star system: Sirius A is the brighter main star and Sirius B is its fainter companion.

Look into the past

When we gaze at the stars, we are peering into the past! The huge distances between us and the stars mean that starlight takes a long time to travel to Earth. For example, the light from Sirius takes around 8.6 years to reach us. This is why we say that it is 8.6 light-years away. Light from our sun reaches the Earth much quicker—in around 8 minutes 20 seconds (8' 20").

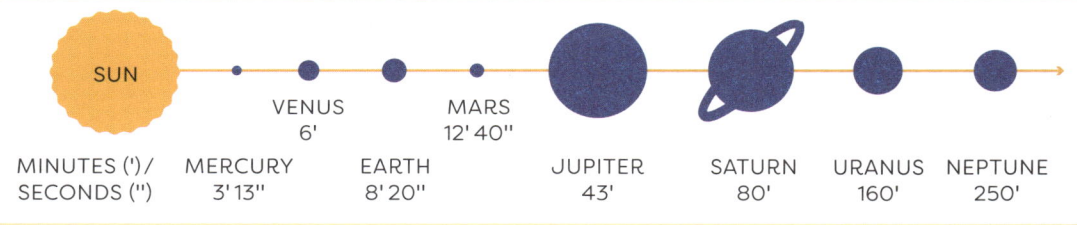

SUN		VENUS 6'		MARS 12' 40"				
MINUTES (') / SECONDS (")	MERCURY 3' 13"		EARTH 8' 20"		JUPITER 43'	SATURN 80'	URANUS 160'	NEPTUNE 250'

Dorrit Hoffleit

The American astronomer **Dorrit Hoffleit** (1907–2007) spent a great deal of time counting the stars that could be seen from Earth with the naked eye. She documented 9,096 and produced a survey titled *Bright Star Catalogue.*

With telescopes, we can now see millions of stars.

Life cycle of a star

How a star changes over time depends on its mass. When stars are massive they exist for a shorter time than ordinary stars because they use up their fuel more quickly. Here, Emma and Louis look at the life cycle of a massive star and an ordinary star.

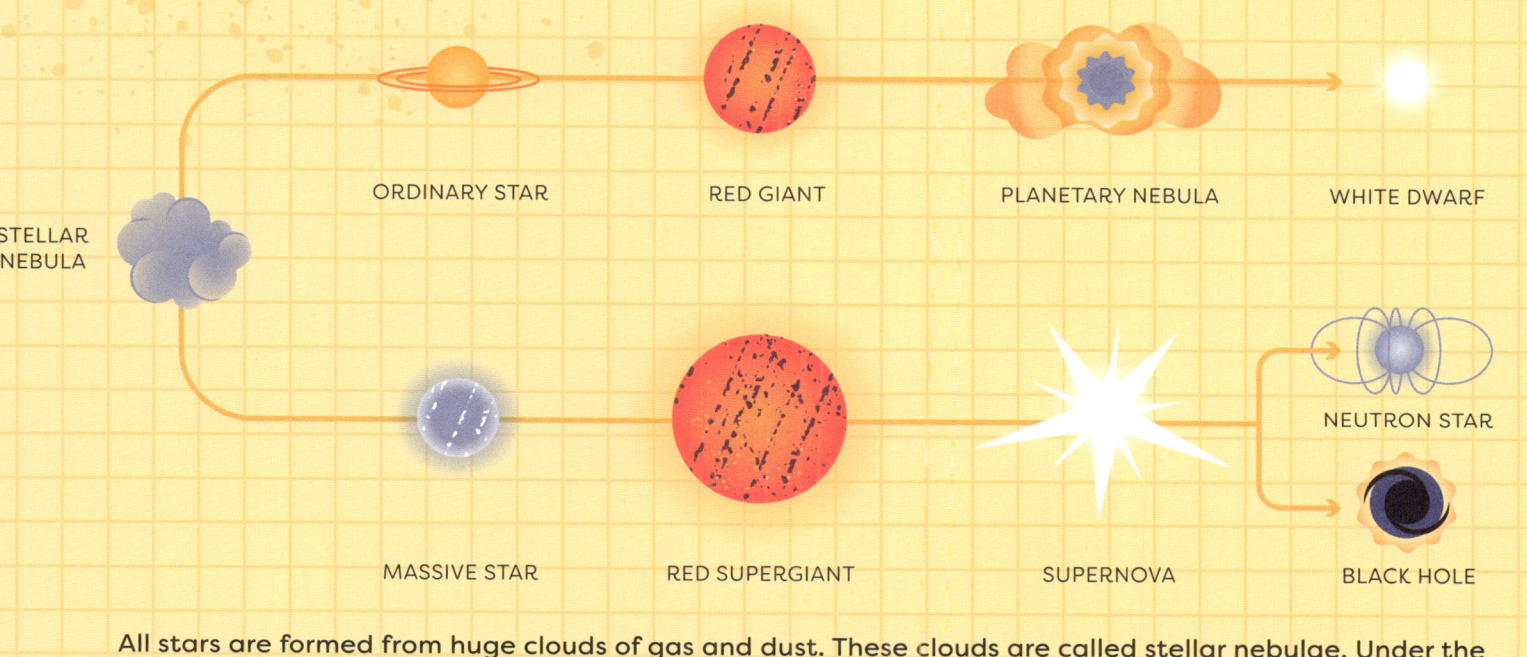

STELLAR NEBULA

ORDINARY STAR

RED GIANT

PLANETARY NEBULA

WHITE DWARF

MASSIVE STAR

RED SUPERGIANT

SUPERNOVA

NEUTRON STAR

BLACK HOLE

All stars are formed from huge clouds of gas and dust. These clouds are called stellar nebulae. Under the influence of gravity, each cloud changes and a protostar is formed. A protostar can develop into either an ordinary star or a massive star. Although stars shine for many thousands and even millions of years, they do not exist forever.

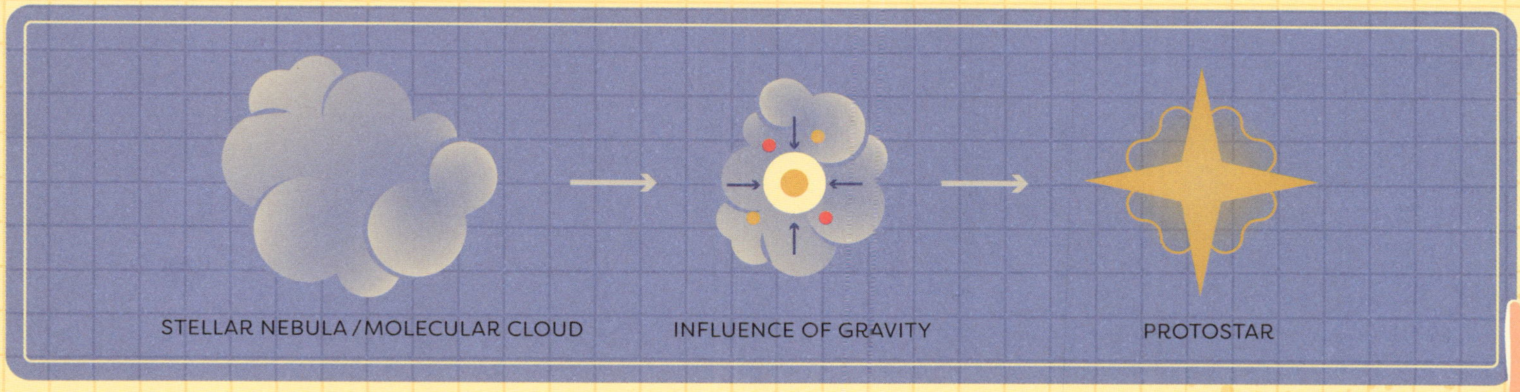

STELLAR NEBULA / MOLECULAR CLOUD

INFLUENCE OF GRAVITY

PROTOSTAR

What Are Galaxies?

At night, you may be able to see a long white streak in the sky. In the past people thought it looked like spilled milk across the darkness—that's how our galaxy, the Milky Way, got its name.

A **galaxy** consists of a collection of stars, planets, and other celestial bodies. Galaxies can be different shapes and sizes. Scientists believe that the universe consists of about 100 billion galaxies, but the number could also be much higher or lower.

It would take a rocket several million years to fly across the entire Milky Way.

As well as our solar system, the Milky Way also contains rogue or **free-floating planets**. These are planets that wander freely through space instead of orbiting a central star.

The **Milky Way** consists of billions of stars. Because it looks like a spiral with several large spiral arms, it is called a spiral galaxy. The sun and the Earth are part of the Milky Way and our entire solar system is located in one of these spiral arms, the Orion Arm.

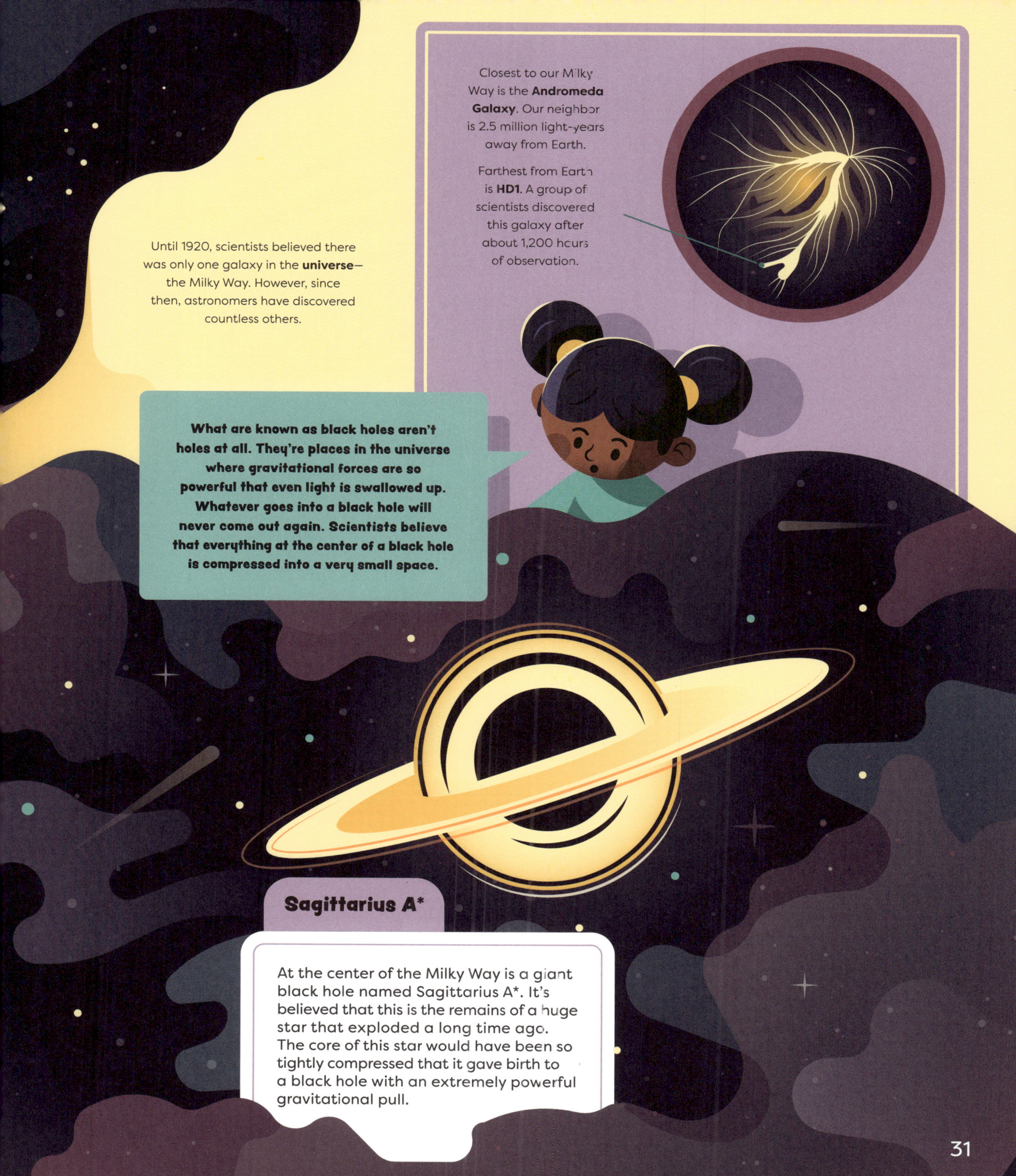

Closest to our Milky Way is the **Andromeda Galaxy**. Our neighbor is 2.5 million light-years away from Earth.

Farthest from Earth is **HD1**. A group of scientists discovered this galaxy after about 1,200 hours of observation.

Until 1920, scientists believed there was only one galaxy in the **universe**—the Milky Way. However, since then, astronomers have discovered countless others.

What are known as black holes aren't holes at all. They're places in the universe where gravitational forces are so powerful that even light is swallowed up. Whatever goes into a black hole will never come out again. Scientists believe that everything at the center of a black hole is compressed into a very small space.

Sagittarius A*

At the center of the Milky Way is a giant black hole named Sagittarius A*. It's believed that this is the remains of a huge star that exploded a long time ago. The core of this star would have been so tightly compressed that it gave birth to a black hole with an extremely powerful gravitational pull.

Looking at Space

For thousands of years, people have used the stars to guide them on their journeys. Today, scientists study space in order to gain a better understanding of the origins and nature of the stars and galaxies. Humans have discovered a great deal about the universe over the past few hundred years.

I think the Earth is the center of the universe. The sun, moon, and stars circle around it.

Wrong! All the planets circle around the sun, not around the Earth.

Thanks to the invention of the telescope, I can see far into space. This shows me that the sun is at the center of our solar system and all celestial bodies move round it.

Aristotle (384 BC–322 BC)

Well over 2,000 years ago, the Greek philosopher Aristotle saw things very differently than we do today. He assumed that the Earth was the center of the universe and that the sun, moon, and stars revolved around it.

Nicolaus Copernicus (1473–1543)

In the 16th century, the astronomer Nicolaus Copernicus observed the movements of the planets and came to a very different conclusion. He realized that they all move around the sun, not the Earth.

Galileo Galilei (1564–1642)

In the 17th century, Galileo Galilei refined the telescope. He confirmed Copernicus's conclusion, as did Johannes Kepler, another astronomer of the day. Kepler noted that planets move in an elliptical shape, not a perfect circle.

I discovered many comets. One was named after me and called Herschel.

CAROLINE HERSCHEL
(1750–1848)

I was recognized as the first professional female astronomer and the king of Denmark gave me a gold medal for my work. The comet I discovered was named after me: Miss Mitchell's Comet.

MARIA MITCHELL
(1818–1889)

I discovered that hydrogen and helium gases are the main components of stars.

CECILIA PAYNE-GAPOSCHKIN
(1900–1979)

Isaac Newton (1643–1727)

In the 17th century, Isaac Newton saw an apple fall from a tree and began to study gravity. He discovered that gravity doesn't just occur on Earth, but that it also affects planets, stars, and galaxies. He formed a law of gravity and showed how it functioned throughout the universe.

Liftoff!

There's a lot to do before astronauts set out on space missions. They even go to swimming pools to train with their equipment to recreate the weightlessness of space.

In space there's virtually no gravity. Astronauts hover instead of standing on the floor of their spacecraft. When they want to go to sleep, they crawl into sleeping bags and tie themselves down with straps so that they won't end up floating around. Water is an extremely useful tool for astronauts preparing for the weightlessness of space: they practice the movements they will carry out in space in specially constructed swimming pools while wearing their space suits.

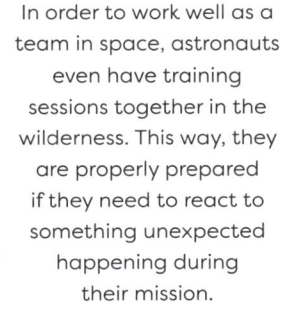

In order to work well as a team in space, astronauts even have training sessions together in the wilderness. This way, they are properly prepared if they need to react to something unexpected happening during their mission.

Building a rocket

A rocket consists of many parts that are situated on top of one another and used in sequence. They're called "stages" and each stage has its own fuel and propellant. As soon as one runs out of fuel, it's discarded into space. These many stages enable the rocket to fly higher and farther, until it finally arrives at its destination in outer space.

Before liftoff, the rocket is loaded with satellites, space probes, and all the equipment the crew will need. And of course the fuel tanks must be full.

Once the order has been given for liftoff, the engines are ignited. They're so powerful that they lift the rocket up into the sky and then counteract Earth's gravitational force.

As it climbs, the rocket accelerates, hurtles through Earth's atmosphere, and enters outer space.

Before each launch, someone from the team on the ground delivers a countdown of the last 10 seconds before liftoff **10–9–8–7–6–5–4–3–2–1–and liftoff!**

People work in the mission control center day and night. Their main task is to maintain contact with the crew in the spacecraft throughout the mission—at launch, during the mission, and until they have landed back on Earth.

If you want to fly into space, you have to be healthy and athletic and have a very good knowledge of physics, medicine, and space technology, among other things.

Astronaut Equipment

The Earth has just the right mix of oxygen, water, air pressure, and light for life to exist. Space has very different conditions, which is why astronauts need special equipment to survive.

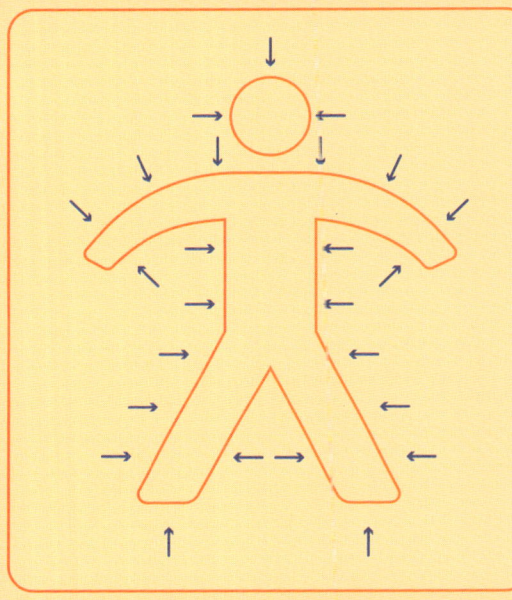

The air around us creates pressure that we are so used to feeling that we barely notice it. However, in space, there's no such pressure—it's like a vacuum. Without protection, our bodies can't survive the harsh conditions, which is why astronauts wear space suits. The suits balance out the pressure and temperature differences, making sure the person inside gets enough oxygen to breathe. The suit isn't just a protective covering—it has lots of technical devices, including ones that allow astronauts to talk to people back on Earth.

The first space suit to be worn by a human in space was called SK-1. The wearer was the Soviet cosmonaut (what the Russians call astronauts) Yuri Gagarin, in 1961, when he orbited the Earth in the space capsule **Vostok 1**. He was the first human to fly into space.

The process of making the suit and the materials used were kept top secret at the time. This was because different countries were competing with each other in their attempts to explore space.

Emma and Louis have uncovered some of the secrets

The SK-1 suit had three layers:

The **outer layer** was like a suit of armor. It provided protection against space dust and harmful rays from the sun.

Rubber and other materials in the **middle layer** helped to keep the pressure in the suit properly balanced.

The **inner layer** was soft and ensured that the wearer would not get too cold.

The helmet protected the head and special tanks took care of the oxygen supply so the cosmonaut could breathe.

Inside the suit was a small radio that the cosmonaut used to keep in touch with the control center on Earth.

The space suit

The **Extravehicular Mobility Unit** (EMU) used by NASA protects astronauts when they leave their spaceship. They do this when they explore celestial bodies or go for a walk in space.

The helmet has a visor that keeps out the intense radiation from the sun.

A rucksack on the back contains different tanks for oxygen, water, and coolant.

The suit consists of several layers that protect the astronaut against the extreme temperatures they will encounter in space.

The central part of the space suit (covering the back and chest) contains everything necessary for survival—oxygen supply, temperature regulator, and apparatus to enable contact with people back on Earth.

Astronauts wear a high-tech diaper that sticks to their skin. Because the space walks take many hours, they cannot go to the bathroom in between. (The longest space walk lasted more than eight hours!)

Special gloves were developed to allow the astronaut to use tools and other equipment in space.

The arms and legs of the suit have several joints so that astronauts can move freely no matter how much equipment they're carrying.

As long as astronauts remain on board their spaceship or space station, they don't have to use an EMU. When they're on board the International Space Station (ISS), the crew members often wear a simple training suit. There are special suits for when they go out into space or return to the Earth's atmosphere.

The boots are thick and tough to protect the astronaut against sharp-edged space dust and micro-meteorites.

Space Explorers

Astronauts are brave people who display remarkable courage as they study and explore space.

Valentina Tereshkova

This Soviet cosmonaut made history as the first woman to travel into space. During her mission aboard Vostok 6 in 1963, she orbited Earth 48 times!

Christina Koch

In 2019, this NASA astronaut spent an incredible 328 days in space. She set the record for the longest time a woman had stayed in space.

Astronauts have to learn and train a lot before they fly out into the universe. It's no easy task being cooped up in a place where there's no gravity and you're far away from your loved ones. Of course the work they do is exciting and important, but they must make many sacrifices and live within a tiny area. Imagine having to stay in your bedroom for hundreds of days!

Gennady Padalka

Until February 2024 this Russian cosmonaut held the record for the longest time spent in space—over five missions, he had been in space for a total of 878 days by the end of 2015 (Oleg Kononenko is expected to reach 1,110 days by the end of September 2024).

Mae Jemison

In 1992, this American doctor flew into space aboard the space shuttle Endeavour. She took plant seeds with her so that she could observe their growth in weightless conditions. Today, space stations such as the ISS can grow lettuce, potatoes, cereals, and other foods.

Neil Armstrong

On July 21, 1969, this American astronaut became the first human to set foot on the moon. He spoke the now-famous words: "That's one small step for a man, one giant leap for mankind."

Chiaki Mukai

This Japanese surgeon journeyed into space in both 1994 and 1998. Her task was to find out how weightlessness affects human bones and muscles.

During the past few decades, space agencies have focused more on the welfare of the animals and adopted a more responsible approach. There are now strict guidelines for how they should be treated.

Animals have also been sent on space missions to test how living organisms react to the special conditions in space. Monkeys, mice, turtles, pigs, fruit flies, bumblebees, caterpillars, ants, and many more have already been sent into space.

The Russian dog Laika was on board the Russian satellite **Sputnik 2** when it circled the Earth in 1957.

Space Stations and Telescopes

Imagine waking up in the morning and looking out of the window at endless space. That is what astronauts do when they're working on board a space station.

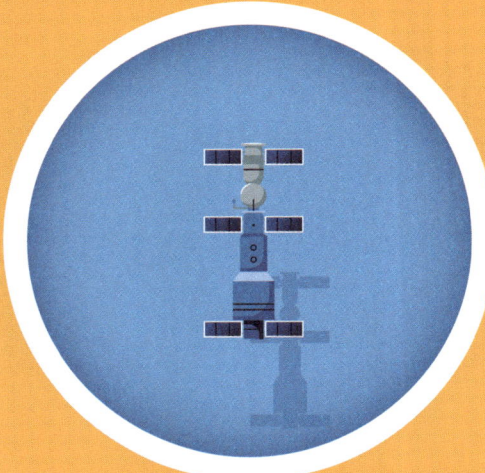

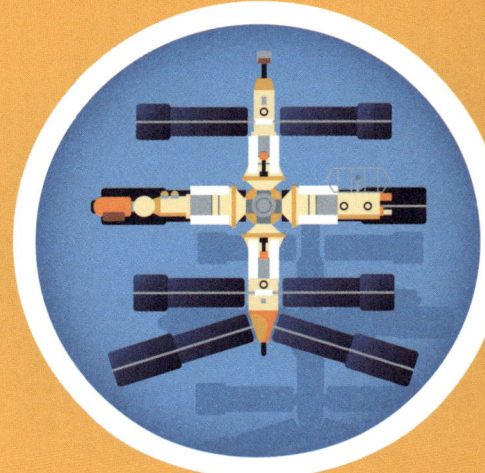

Salyut 1 was the first space station. It was launched by the Soviet Union in 1971 and remained in operation for just one year. Its equipment included telescopes to observe the stars and a solar observatory to study the activities of the sun.

Skylab was the first US space station, and astronauts lived and worked on it in 1973 and 1974. The crews changed regularly and would stay for a few months at a time. In 1979, NASA guided Skylab back into the Earth's atmosphere to prevent it from falling on populated areas. It broke apart over the Indian Ocean, ending its mission safely.

Mir, the Soviet (later Russian) space station, allowed scientists to live and work in space for longer periods of time. It orbited Earth from 1986 until 2001. Scientists from different countries, including the USA, Canada, Japan, France, and of course Russia, worked on Mir. Norman Thagard was the first American scientist to work there.

The British chemist Helen Sharman was the first British person and the first woman to visit the Mir space station, in 1991.

Space telescopes are telescopes specially designed to explore space. They have features that allow them to see beyond the Earth's atmosphere. Emma and Louis have actually seen some of them.

The **Hubble Space Telescope** has made it possible to obtain the first images of galaxies beyond our Milky Way—for example, the Andromeda Galaxy (the Milky Way's nearest neighbor). Scientists have learned a great deal more about the universe thanks to this new kind of telescope.

- The Hubble Space Telescope orbits the Earth at a distance of 326 miles (525 kilometers) above the Earth's surface.
- NASA transported the telescope into outer space in 1990.
- Every few years, space shuttle missions are launched to test the telescope's equipment. NASA scientists are then able to add new, improved instruments and carry out any necessary repairs.

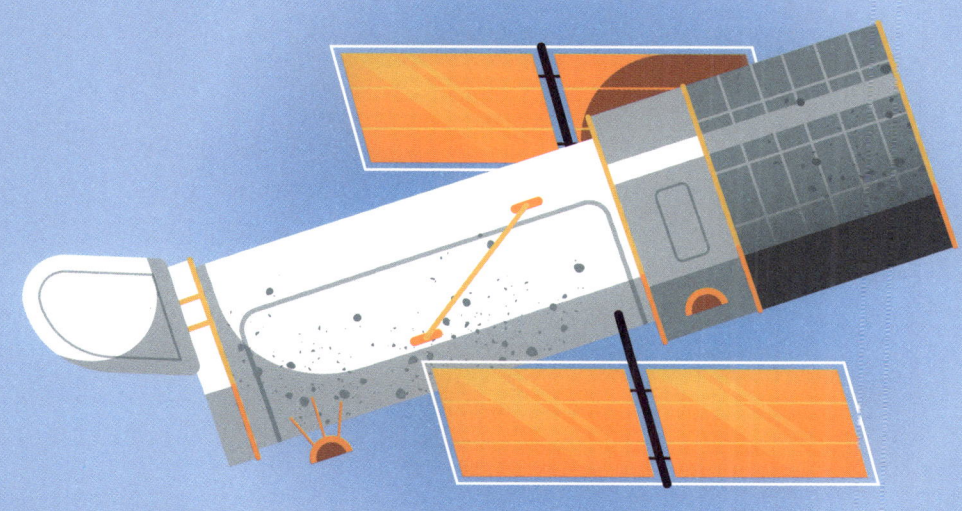

Chandra X-ray Observatory

The Chandra X-ray telescope acts a bit like a detective, locating X-ray emissions from different regions in the universe. These rays are invisible to the naked eye, but they provide important insights into black holes and supernova explosions.

James Webb Telescope

Since 2022, the **James Webb Space Telescope** has been orbiting the sun around 930,000 miles (1.5 million kilometers) from the Earth. It captures images of the infrared regions of light, which are also invisible to the naked eye, allowing us to study the formation of new stars and planets in distant parts of the universe.

Living on the International Space Station

There are astronauts from many different countries living and working together on the International Space Station (ISS). They show just how much can be achieved when people work with, and not against, one another.

The **ISS** is made up of many modules, with a wide variety of fittings and equipment. Think of it as a house that has been gradually built by different space agencies from different countries since 1998. These countries include the USA (NASA), Russia (Roscosmos), Japan (JAXA), Canada (CSA), and the European Union (ESA).

In order to live and work together in harmony, all the astronauts must learn to speak English and Russian.

Supersized space lab

Today the ISS is bigger than a football pitch. It is a completely unique structure, not just because of its large size, but also because it has provided amazing opportunites for research.

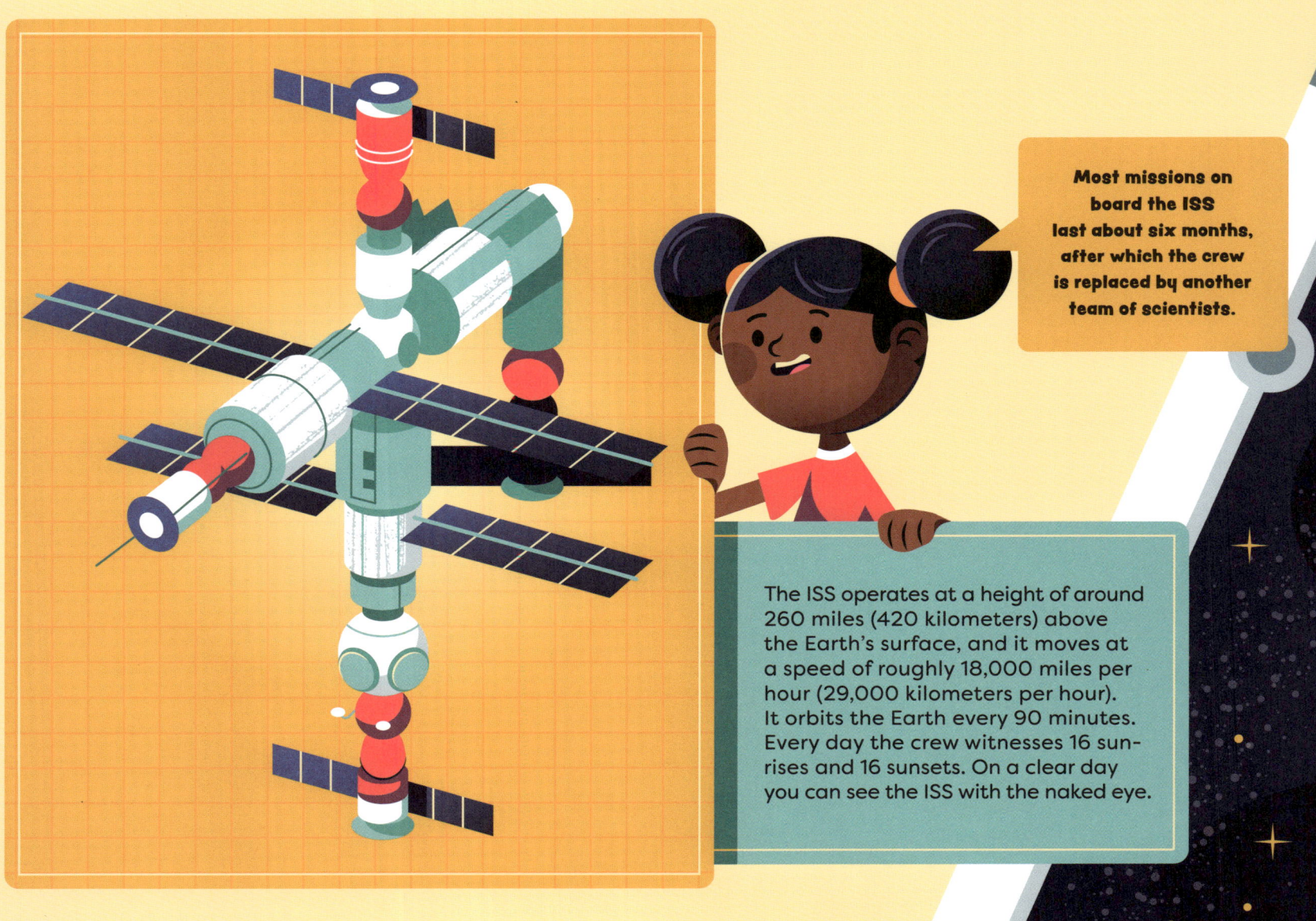

Most missions on board the ISS last about six months, after which the crew is replaced by another team of scientists.

The ISS operates at a height of around 260 miles (420 kilometers) above the Earth's surface, and it moves at a speed of roughly 18,000 miles per hour (29,000 kilometers per hour). It orbits the Earth every 90 minutes. Every day the crew witnesses 16 sunrises and 16 sunsets. On a clear day you can see the ISS with the naked eye.

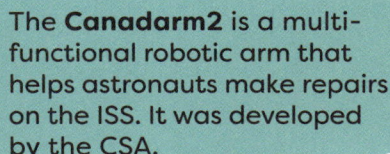

The **Canadarm2** is a multi-functional robotic arm that helps astronauts make repairs on the ISS. It was developed by the CSA.

The **Destiny** module, the fourth American laboratory on the ISS, contains the **Veggie Facility**. Here, the crew grows plants using special bags filled with nutrients and LED lights (as there is no sunlight). They study plant growth in weightless conditions and also eat them for their own health! Similar experiments are being carried out on the Japanese **Kibo** module and the European **Columbus Space Laboratory**.

Of course, the crew members also have to go to the toilet in space. They go the same way as they do on Earth, but with the aid of air currents and special vacuum technology the waste is sucked into special bags, which keeps the spacecraft clean and hygienic.

NASA has developed a very special toilet for the ISS. It cost around $23 million! What is so special about it? Almost 90 percent of the urine can be recycled into pure drinking water. It's an ingenious way of maintaining the water supply while in space.

In space, most of the food has to be freeze-dried. It must be highly nutritious because astronauts need a lot of fuel to do their work.

As with any job on Earth, astronauts have working hours and time off. To relax, they might read books, watch movies, communicate with people on Earth, or simply gaze out of the window. The views are not quite the same as the ones they get back home!

Spacecraft

It would not be possible to explore the universe without spacecraft and vehicles. Here, Emma and Louis take a look at some of the vehicles that have been, or still have, active roles in important missions.

Space probes

Space probes are uncrewed craft used to obtain information from outer space and send it back to Earth.

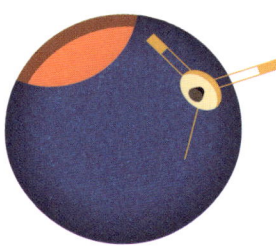

In 2007, **Chang'e 1** was the first Chinese probe to reach the moon. Four more missions followed, with the last one, **Chang'e 5** (launched in November 2020), bringing back samples collected from the moon.

NASA's **Voyager 1** and **Voyager 2** were launched in 1977 and are still gathering important data for space research. They are a long way away from our sun and its gravitational pull. These are unmanned space probes.

In 2015, NASA's space probe **New Horizons** circled the dwarf planet Pluto, photographing its surface. The pictures showed features such as ravines and mountains of nitrogen ice.

The space probes **Pioneer 10** and **11**, also NASA's, reached the outskirts of our solar system in 1972 and 1973. Pioneer 10 actually reached the very point at which the sun's force of gravity began to weaken—a major success in the history of space exploration.

The space probe **Cassini-Huygens**, which could be controlled remotely, took about seven years to reach Saturn and its moons. It remained there for 13 years, collecting information. One of its discoveries was that water pours from a crack in the icy covering of Saturn's moon Enceladus. In 2005, the land probe Huygens was the first spacecraft to land on a moon other than our own. This landing, on Saturn's moon Titan, was a technological triumph!

Space shuttle program

NASA's **space shuttle Discovery** undertook an incredible 39 missions! The whole space shuttle program lasted 30 years in total. Over this period, five space shuttles were built and not all of their flights were crewed. Their missions included putting satellites, space probes, and telescopes into the Earth's orbit.

What happens to a launch rocket when it has completed its task?

Most of the time, the different parts simply burn up in the Earth's atmosphere, under the direction of the space agency that launched the rocket. This process is very important as it stops anything falling onto any populated areas. Instead it falls into the ocean or onto places far away from people. However, there is also a lot of debris floating around in space, such as bits of rockets or satellites that are no longer functioning. Today, space agencies are trying hard to avoid creating space junk.

Mars rovers

Curiosity and **Perseverance** are remotely controlled rovers that have been sent to Mars to find out whether it is possible for life to survive there. They are looking for signs of past life and have found salt deposits, which might provide evidence of this as microorganisms often live in salt water on the Earth. There are also signs that there was once water on Mars.

Exoplanets

The discovery of exoplanets has changed our whole concept of the universe. Could there be life in other planetary systems? Many scientists are trying to find an answer to this fascinating question—and so are Emma and Louis!

Exoplanets are planets outside our own solar system. "Exo" is Greek for "outside."

Exoplanets orbit stars in solar systems just like ours, but they are a huge distance away from Earth.

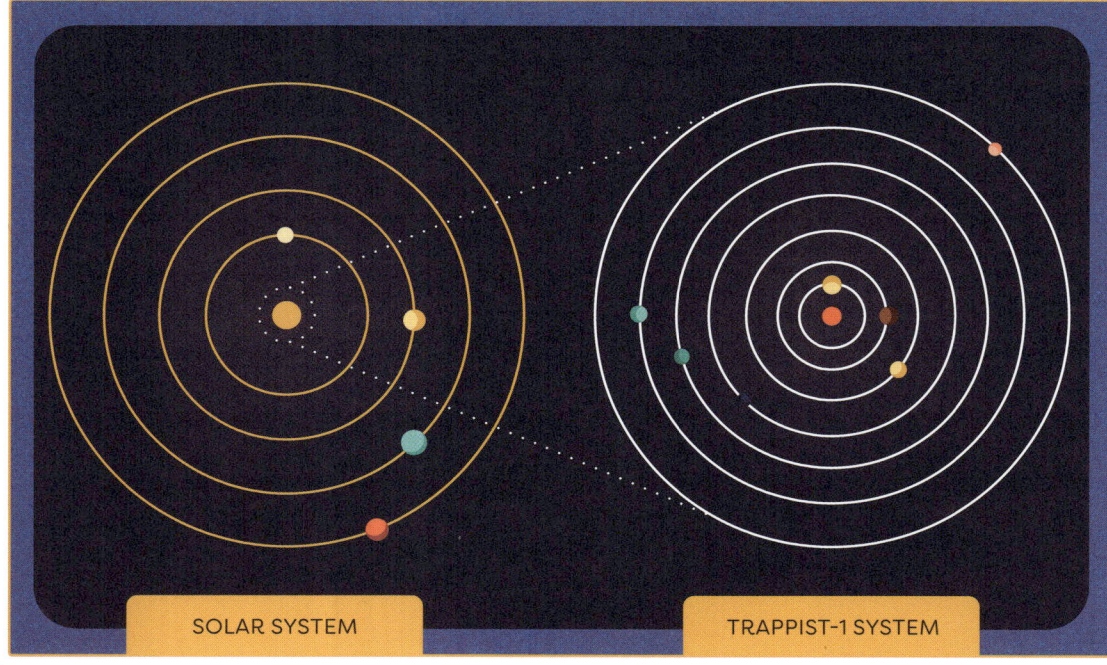

SOLAR SYSTEM

TRAPPIST-1 SYSTEM

The **Trappist-1** solar system is about 40 light-years away from Earth and is situated in our galaxy, the Milky Way.

Its name comes from the **Trappist Telescope** (Transiting Planets and Planetesimals Small Telescope), which made the discovery. The Trappist-1 solar system has seven orbiting exoplanets.

Astronomers study the stars very closely to see if there are exoplanets orbiting them. For example, if a star is seen to be gently rocking forward and backward, it could mean that there's an exoplanet close by. That's because it could be exerting its own force of gravity on the star.

The planet **Kepler-16b** orbits two stars. It is also known as the "Tatooine planet" because the fictional planet Tatooine that features in the *Star Wars* films has two suns.

JUPITER

In 1995, **51 Pegasi b**, or **Dimidium**, was the first exoplanet to be discovered outside our solar system. This was an important advance in our exploration of the universe. Until then, there had been no proof that there might be planets orbiting stars in other systems.

The exoplanet **WASP-39 b** is a gas giant. Researchers also call it **hot Saturn** because it has roughly the same mass as that planet. It was discovered in 2011 and is 700 light-years away from Earth.

HD 209458 b is also known as **Osiris**. With the aid of the Hubble Space Telescope, scientists have detected large quantities of water vapor in this exoplanet's atmosphere, which could mean that there is water on it.

EARTH

The exoplanet **Kepler-186f** was discovered in 2014. Scientists believe it contains water, a vital precondition for life on any planet.

Space Tourism

If you want to leave the Earth's atmosphere, you don't necessarily have to be an astronaut. There are also space tourists—and that makes Emma and Louis quite curious.

The American Dennis Tito was the first tourist to go into space. He visited in 2001. The first female spaceflight participant to go was Anousheh Ansari, an Iranian American electrical engineer, in 2006.

The first tourists traveled on the Russian spacecraft **Soyuz** to the ISS and generally stayed there for one or two weeks.

Prospective tourists must undergo intensive training before they visit the ISS. For example, they have to learn how to communicate with the control center on Earth, how to put on a space suit, and what to do in an emergency.

The New Shepard

The US space flight system New Shepard consists of a space capsule and a carrier rocket. Up to six people can travel into space in it. At an altitude of around 25 miles (40 kilometers), the capsule detaches and flies on to an altitude of around 62 miles (100 kilometers)—the Kármán line. Once there, it orbits briefly in weightlessness before landing back on Earth with the help of a parachute. The flight takes around 11 minutes in total.

In 2021, the New Shepard carried people into space for the first time. One of the four who went was 82-year-old American Wally Funk. This was a big dream come true for her: Funk had trained to be an astronaut in 1961 and applied to NASA several times, but she had never made it into space in all those years.

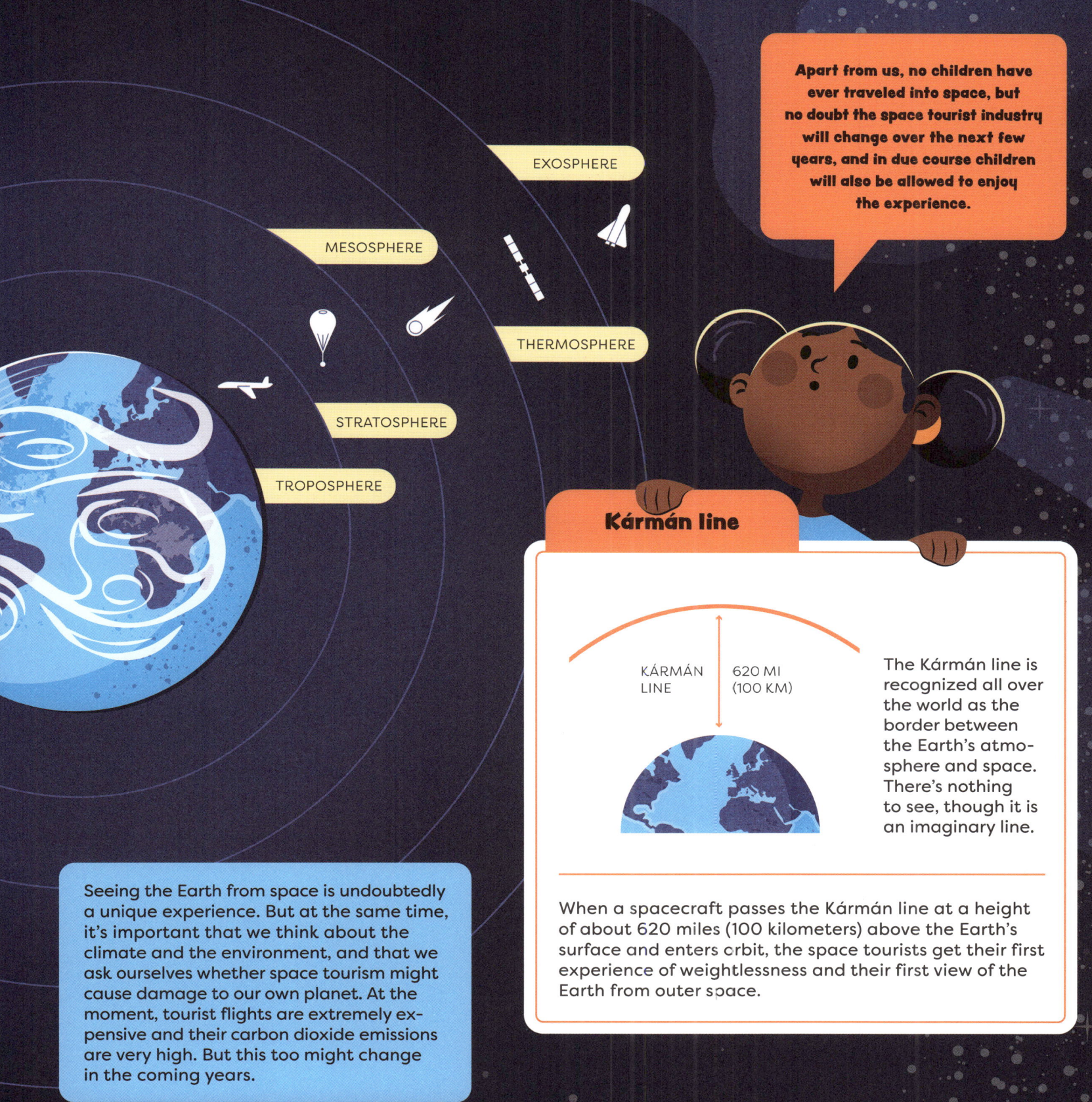

EXOSPHERE

MESOSPHERE

THERMOSPHERE

STRATOSPHERE

TROPOSPHERE

Apart from us, no children have ever traveled into space, but no doubt the space tourist industry will change over the next few years, and in due course children will also be allowed to enjoy the experience.

Kármán line

KÁRMÁN LINE

620 MI (100 KM)

The Kármán line is recognized all over the world as the border between the Earth's atmosphere and space. There's nothing to see, though it is an imaginary line.

When a spacecraft passes the Kármán line at a height of about 620 miles (100 kilometers) above the Earth's surface and enters orbit, the space tourists get their first experience of weightlessness and their first view of the Earth from outer space.

Seeing the Earth from space is undoubtedly a unique experience. But at the same time, it's important that we think about the climate and the environment, and that we ask ourselves whether space tourism might cause damage to our own planet. At the moment, tourist flights are extremely expensive and their carbon dioxide emissions are very high. But this too might change in the coming years.

Space Stories

The human imagination has been inspired by the sight of stars in the night sky for a long time, perhaps because of their beauty—or perhaps because they remind us that we know so little about the universe.

There are countless movies and TV series that take place in distant galaxies, such as **Star Trek**, **Star Wars**, and **2001: A Space Odyssey**.

MISTER SPOCK FROM **STAR TREK**

LUKE SKYWALKER FROM **STAR WARS**

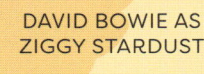

DAVID BOWIE AS ZIGGY STARDUST

Musicians have been inspired by space, too. Gustav Holst's **The Planets** is a popular classical piece, and there are well-known songs that explore space themes, like David Bowie's **Space Oddity**, Elton John's **Rocket Man**, and The Beatles' **Across the Universe**.

Artists have also been fascinated by the universe, and Emma and Louis have seen some of their works, like Vincent van Gogh's **The Starry Night** (1989), Max Ernst's **A moon is good things** (1970), and Yayoi Kusama's **The Souls of Millions of Light Years Away** (2013). Their works give us the feeling that we are gazing into the infinity of the universe.

The Hitchhiker's Guide to the Galaxy by Douglas Adams describes the space adventure of a man named Arthur Dent. In the story, aliens are building a highway through the universe and to do so must destroy Earth. Arthur explores the universe with Ford Prefect, an alien, as he works on his hitchhikes through space and writes his travel guide.

Flash Gordon by Alex Raymond is a comic named after its main character. With his friends, Flash Gordon defends the Earth from the dastardly Emperor Ming, who seeks to rule the universe.

Guardians of the Galaxy by Arnold Drake and Gene Colan is another comic about defending the universe from evil forces. The characters include a talking raccoon called Rocket and a treelike character named Groot.

Paul Atreides is the main character in Frank Herbert's book **Dune**. In the story, Paul is defending the desertlike planet Arrakis, where an important spice called melange is found. This spice is important throughout the universe as it enables space travel and gives people special abilities. Because of this, many people want power over Arrakis.

Goodbye, Space!

Emma and Louis have finished their space adventure for now! They've glimpsed distant galaxies, learned about our solar system, and explored all kinds of planets. They were both super-impressed by Jupiter's many moons and the research being carried out on Mars.

It's amazing how much humans have learned about our solar system in just the past few decades. Thanks to modern space telescopes, we can look forward to solving even more of the universe's mysteries!

It has become very clear to Emma and Louis that there is still so much we don't know. How exciting! Our understanding of space has only really just begun—there are black holes and exoplanets just waiting to be investigated in the near future.

Glossary

Asteroids
These are mostly made of rock, with a smaller proportion of metals and sometimes ice. They are the remnants from the early stages of our solar system, when solid materials came together to form the planets. Asteroids were bits and pieces that were not big enough to become planets. There are millions of asteroids between the orbits of Mars and Jupiter, and this region is known as the asteroid belt.

Astronaut
A person who has been specially trained to travel and work in space. The Russian word is cosmonaut, and the Chinese is taikonaut.

Atmosphere
A layer of gases surrounding a celestial object, such as a planet, held in place by the object's gravity.

Atom
An atom is the smallest unit of nature. Everything consists of these tiny particles.

Carbon
A chemical element. Coal, diamonds and pencil lead are made of carbon. Carbon bonds well and is therefore found in all living things.

Carbon dioxide
Carbon dioxide is one of the gases that make up the Earth's atmosphere. It has no color or smell. Human activities like the burning of fossil fuels increase carbon dioxide levels. This changes our climate because it exceeds the normal amount for our atmosphere.

Climate
The long-term weather conditions (such as temperature, rainfall, and wind levels) in a particular place over time. The Earth's climate depends mainly on its proximity to the equator.

Comet
A celestial body consisting of rock, dust, and frozen gases that orbits the sun. When it goes close to the sun, it develops a shining tail.

Crater
A crater is a hole on the surface of a planet or moon, and can be formed by the impact of meteorites, asteroids, or comets. Craters can take various shapes and forms. For example, on Earth, volcanoes often form funnel-shaped craters.

Dwarf planets
These are celestial bodies that orbit the sun, just like regular planets, but they are smaller. They also share space with other celestial bodies and do not dominate their orbits. In our solar system, Pluto is a dwarf planet that orbits the sun. Its diameter is 1,477 miles (2,377 kilometers).

Energy
Energy is all around us, even though we can't see or touch it. It's the power that enables us to move objects and our own body. There are many different forms of energy: for example, if it's used for movement, we call it kinetic energy, while the heat of the sun is called thermal energy.

Exoplanets
Planets that orbit stars outside our solar system.

Gravity
An invisible force that attracts objects with mass toward one another. Gravity is the reason objects fall to the ground instead of floating in the air, planets orbit the sun, and moons orbit planets.

Helium
An odorless, colorless noble gas that is lighter than air. Incidentally, there is helium in airships and some party balloons.

Hydrogen
An odorless, colorless gas that burns quickly. It is found in all living things on Earth—water is made up of hydrogen and oxygen—but also in the stars and gas clouds in the universe.

Matter
Our world is made of matter—everything you can touch is matter. But the air we breathe is also matter. There is also matter in the universe, including planets, moons, and comets. A space in which there is no matter is called a vacuum.

Meteorite
A chunk of rock that enters the Earth's atmosphere. Small ones burn up, but larger ones sometimes crash into the Earth.

Moons
Natural satellites that orbit celestial bodies such as planets, dwarf planets, asteroids, and comets.

Names of the planets

Apart from the Earth, all the planets in our solar system were named after Roman deities. For example, *Mars* was named after the god of war because the red exterior is reminiscent of the color of blood. *Jupiter,* the largest planet in the solar system, was named after the king of the gods. The god *Saturn,* who, according to legend, was defeated by his son Jupiter, became the namesake of the sixth planet from the sun due to its slower orbit than Jupiter. Due to its bluish color, *Neptune* was named after the god of the sea and, as *Venus* reflects the most light and appears the brightest of all the planets, it was named after the goddess of beauty. *Mercury,* the fastest planet in our solar system, bears the name of the messenger of the gods, who, according to legend, can move faster than light. Finally, presumably because of its light blue color, the planet *Uranus* bears the name of the sky god.

Nitrogen

An invisible gas that has no smell. It makes up by far the largest proportion of gas in the Earth's atmosphere and in the air we breathe (about 78 percent).

Nutrients

Foods that help plants, animals, and humans to live, grow, and be healthy.

Organism

Any living thing.

Oxygen

Like nitrogen, oxygen has no smell and is invisible. About 21 percent of the Earth's atmosphere consists of oxygen, and we inhale it every time we take a breath. It's essential for the survival of all plants, animals, and humans.

Planets

Spherical celestial bodies that orbit a star (such as our sun). They can be made of solid materials or gases. There are also free-floating planets. These are planets that wander freely through space instead of orbiting a central star.

Plasma

A mixture of particles that has electrical and magnetic properties. It can conduct electricity.

Auroras (polar lights)

Small electrically charged particles from the sun that glow red, green, blue, and violet when they mix with the air in the Earth's atmosphere. This magical celestial glow occurs mainly in the areas around the South and North poles.

Rocket

A launch vehicle with engines that are powerful enough to propel craft beyond the Earth's atmosphere and enter space.

Space

Space can mean something empty that can be filled, like a shelf for books. However it can also refer to the universe, where planets and other celestial bodies move around. It includes Earth and everything else.

Stars

Celestial bodies that shine and consist mainly of hot gas.

Sulfur

A chemical element that is yellowish and has a strong odor.

Telescope

An instrument used in astronomy that collects and focuses light to show stars and planets magnified.

Time

Time helps us to measure the gap between events. We can distinguish between what happened in the past, what is happening now, and what will happen in the future. It forms a very long chain of events. As long as 3,500 years ago, ancient Egyptians were already using sundials and calendars in order to measure time.

Weightlessness

The state in which there is no apparent gravitational force pulling things (or people) downwards. This state occurs in space, where the force of attraction is much weaker than on Earth, making things float.

Exploring Space
Adventures Across the Universe with Emma and Louis

Written by Anne Ameri-Siemens
Illustrated by Anton Hallmann

This book was conceived, edited, and designed by Little Gestalten

Edited by Robert Klanten, Fay Evans and Friederike Christoph

Translation from German by David Wilson

Layout by Melanie Ullrich

Typefaces: Calcine by Mark Frömberg, Filson Soft by Olivier Gourvat, Peachy Keen JF by Jason Walcott

Printed by Print Best OÜ
Made in Estonia

Published by Little Gestalten, Berlin, 2024
ISBN 978-3-96704-770-7

For more information, and to order books, please visit: gestalten.com/collections/little-gestalten

Bibliographic information published by the Deutsche Nationalbibliothek. The Deutsche Nationalbibliothek lists this publication in the Deutsche Nationalbibliografie; detailed bibliographic data are available online at dnb.de.

This book was printed on paper certified according to the standards of the FSC®.

Explore other titles from the series!

Explore the World
Discoveries That Shaped Our World

ISBN: 978-3-96704-703-5

Explore the Rainforest
Emma and Louis in the Jungle

ISBN: 978-3-96704-719-6

Explore the Ocean
Adventures Under the Sea with Emma and Louis

ISBN: 978-3-96704-750-9

Anne Ameri-Siemens is an award-winning writer who tells whimsical stories about the world around us. After working for Frankfurter Allgemeine Sonntagszeitung, she wrote a Spiegel Bestseller. Anne lives in Berlin but would like to spend some time in space. *Exploring Space* is her fourth book with Little Gestalten.

Anton Hallmann was born in Brandenburg, Germany, and studied illustration at the Hamburg University of Applied Sciences. He currently lives in Stockholm and is primarily working in editorial illustration for newspapers and magazines. *Exploring Space* is also his fourth book with Little Gestalten.